Then she realized there were so many things that happened before Flurry Heart was born, though, and the royal baby would never get to experience them, and that made Pinkie sad.

But then Pinkie Pie had the **BEST IDEA EVER.** "I'm going to make you a book about all the amazing things you missed and all the amazing things you get to look forward to!" Pinkie continued, "I call it…"

This book belongs to:

Baby Flurry Heart

From:

Pinkie Pie

5-Minute Stories

Cover design by Carolyn Bull.

Little, Brown and Company
Hachette Book Group
1290 Avenue of the Americas, New York, NY 10104
Visit us at LBYR.com
mylittlepony.com

First Edition: October 2017

Little, Brown and Company is a division of Hachette Book Group, Inc.
The Little, Brown name and logo are trademarks of Hachette Book Group, Inc.

The publisher is not responsible for websites (or their content) that are not owned by the publisher.

Library of Congress Control Number 2017935524

ISBN: 978-0-316-55731-3 (paper over board), 978-0-316-44486-6 (ebook), 978-0-316-44488-0 (ebook), 978-0-316-44485-9 (ebook)

Printed in China

APS

10 9 8 7 6 5 4 3 2 1

Licensed By:

My Little Pony

5-Minute Stories

By Pinkie Pie

Adapted by Magnolia Belle

Little, Brown and Company

New York · Boston

STORIES!

THE ROYAL WEDDING

AKA THE CRAZIEST WEDDING EVER!

When two ponies **FALL IN LOVE**, they get married and have a **WEDDING.**

It's a **GINORMOUS** party with rings and dancing and a **GREAT BIG CAKE** with two ponies on top. Not real ponies. They're little toy ponies.

When Princess Cadance and Shining Armor got married, it was one of the BIGGEST weddings Canterlot had ever seen.

Ponies came from all over Equestria and everypony was

SUPER EXCITED!

Well, not EVERYpony.

PRINCESS TWILIGHT SPARKLE was not excited at all. Shining Armor was her big brother, and she was **UPSET** because she didn't even know that he was planning to get married.

She thought a sister should get to find out before everypony else.

Twilight's sadness about the wedding didn't last long. Once she realized her brother was going to marry Princess Cadance, she completely changed her mind and

FLIPPED OUT WITH EXCITEMENT.

Twilight Sparkle loved Princess Cadance. She had known her all her life and already felt like she was family. Princess Cadance used to foal-sit Twilight when she was very young. Twilight could not wait to have Princess Cadance as her new BIG SISTER.

Since Princess Twilight Sparkle LOVED Shining Armor and Princess Cadance so much, she wanted their wedding to be SPECTACULAR. She gathered all her closest friends, including Fluttershy, Pinkie Pie, Applejack, Rainbow Dash, Rarity, and Spike, and asked for their help to make it the

BEST WEDDING EVER.

They all packed up and took the **FRIENDSHIP EXPRESS** to Canterlot.

On the big day of the wedding, everything seemed perfect. Then it turned out that Princess Cadance wasn't really Princess Cadance. She was **CHRYSALIS**, queen of the Changelings, **IN DISGUISE!**

Chrysalis put a SPELL on Shining Armor. She was going to soak up his love and use it as power to rule over all Equestria.

With her scary Changelings by her side, she would be

UNSTOPPABLE.

Twilight Sparkle and the other ponies **TRIED TO STOP** Chrysalis, but the Changelings were just **TOO STRONG**.

They overpowered the ponies with their strength and numbers.

The ponies needed something EVEN STRONGER to defeat Chrysalis.

They found what they were looking for—Shining Armor and Princess Cadance's **TRUE LOVE!** Shining Armor broke the spell by **TOUCHING HORNS** with the real Princess Cadance.

KA-POW

The SHOCK WAVE OF LOVE was so POWERFUL, it BLASTED Chrysalis and all her Changelings back to the Changeling Kingdom.

With Chrysalis gone, Shining Armor and Princess Cadance were finally able to have their wedding.

And there were rings and dancing and a
GREAT BIG CAKE
with two little ponies on top.

It was the BEST.
WEDDING.
EVER!

FOAL-SITTING 101

AKA BEST WORKOUT EVER!

Moms and dads are pretty busy ponies, and they aren't always able to spend every minute of every day with their foals. There are places they have to go, like jobs and fancy dinners with other moms and dads.

That's where **FOAL-SITTERS** come in.

Foal-sitters are **NOT** ponies
who sit on little colts and fillies.
HA-HA!

They are ponies who make sure little colts and fillies have everything they need while their parents are away. They help the foals feel safe and warm, and sometimes they even help them...

HAVE FUN.

Foal-sitting is no trot in the park. There are lots and lots of

RESPONSIBILITIES.

Pinkie Pie knows foal-sitting is intense, and that **STRETCHING** and WARMING UP beforehoof is important.

Foal-sitters have to be on their games and ready.
As soon as Mom and Dad leave, anything can happen.

Sometimes when foals get upset, it means they're hungry. Be careful.

Feeding time can get

MESSY!

And sometimes there is CRYING.

After feeding, bath time is a must. It's usually fun with all the **BUBBLES** and bath toys.

But sometimes there is **CRYING.**

But don't worry! Foal-sitting is not *all* crying.
There are also

DIRTY DIAPERS.

And then it is time for bed. A foal-sitter's job doesn't end at bedtime. Little fillies and colts need to be tucked in so sweetly. A good

also doesn't hurt when putting them to rest.

Did you know baby ponies can start flying and using **MAGIC** very early on? They can get into all sorts of things, and foal-sitters have to really keep an eye on them.

Foal-sitting is definitely a lot of work. Little foals might be a hoof-ful sometimes and can wear a pony out. And sometimes there is

CRYING.

But just ask Pinkie—at the end of the day, when a foal-sitter knows she has made an impression, it makes it...

ALL WORTH IT.

ALL ABOUT ALICORNS

AKA HORNS + WINGS = MAGIC!

Ponies in Equestria come in all SHAPES, COLORS, AND SIZES. The kinds of ponies they are determine how they shape the world around them.

There are **EARTH PONIES,** who get their

STRENGTH FROM
THE LAND.

Earth ponies have a special **CONNECTION TO NATURE.** They love plants and animals.

There are the WINGED PEGASI, who soar
through the skies and CONTROL THE WEATHER.

They like to feel the wind beneath their wings and **FLY FREE.**

There are **UNICORNS,** who can use their horns to perform **GREAT MAGIC.**

With their magic, they can **LEVITATE** and make **THINGS APPEAR** from nowhere. Sometimes they even use

MAGIC
FOR PRANKS.

Then there is a very special kind of pony called an **ALICORN**. Alicorns have cute **HORNS** and adorable **WINGS**. Very few ponies have both. That makes

ALICORNS SUPER RARE.

In fact, Flurry Heart was the first one ever born!

Other known ALICORNS in Equestria are:

Princess Cadance

Princess Celestia

Princess Twilight Sparkle

Princess Luna

Alicorns have elements of all different kinds of ponies. They use **MAGIC** like Unicorns.

They **FLY** through the sky like Pegasi. And they can get **POWER FROM THE LAND** like Earth ponies. That makes them

SUPER SPECIAL.

Being an Alicorn also means that they have a

HUGE RESPONSIBILITY.

Alicorns are DESTINED for

BIG THINGS.

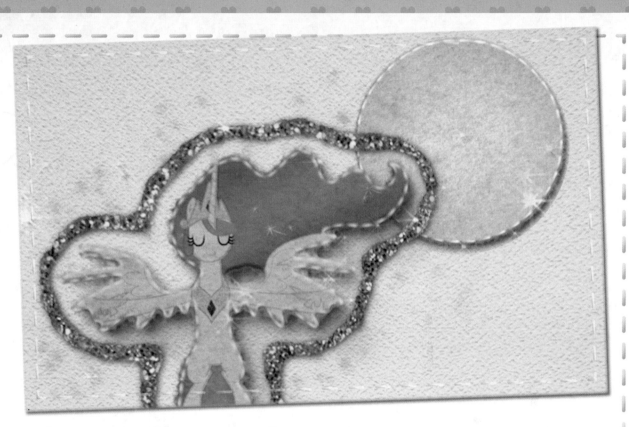

Princess Celestia and Princess Luna are responsible for **RAISING THE SUN AND THE MOON** every single day. That is no small feat!

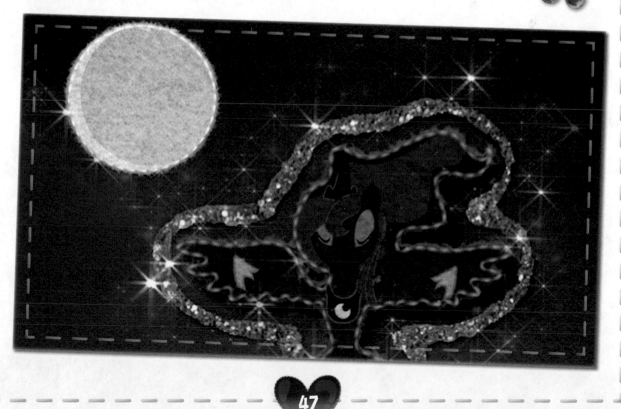

Princess Cadance rules the Crystal Empire and uses her magic to spread **LOVE** across the land. She **SHARES KINDNESS** and **GOODWILL** everywhere she goes.

Princess Twilight uses the

ELEMENTS OF HARMONY

and the **MAGIC OF FRIENDSHIP** to protect all Equestria. She gets a little help from her awesome friends, of course.

That means that one day baby Flurry Heart is going to do something PRETTY AMAZING, too.

Nopony knows how yet, but one day, **BABY FLURRY HEART** is going to

CHANGE THE WORLD.

CUTIE MARK MAGIC

AKA WHY IS MY FLANK BLANK?

As ponies grow up, one of the most amazing things that happens to them is getting their CUTIE MARK. It's a wonderful and magical experience that everypony goes through.

Cutie Marks are special marks on a pony's flank that show the world who they are and what they love doing. All ponies are **BORN WITHOUT CUTIE MARKS.**

CUTIE MARKS MAGICALLY APPEAR when ponies discover what makes them **UNIQUE.**

Pinkie Pie's cutie mark is a set of three **BALLOONS**. That's because she **LOVES PARTIES** and making **OTHER PONIES HAPPY!**

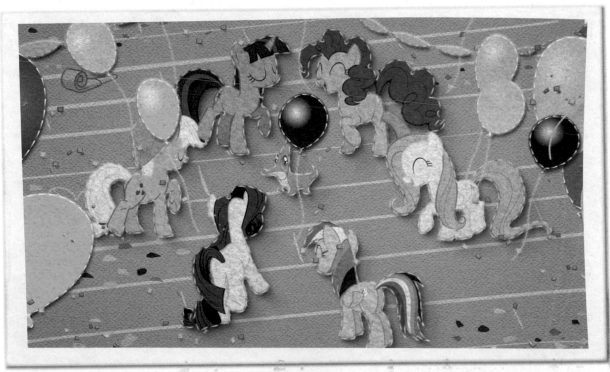

The anticipation a pony feels before he or she finally gets a cutie mark can drive some ponies crazy. Sometimes they have **LOTS OF QUESTIONS** about it.

Some ponies get their CUTIE MARKS EARLY, when they are VERY YOUNG.

Others can get them much later.

It can be **SUPER STRESSFUL** for a pony to not know what his or her cutie mark is going to be. Some ponies try anything and everything to **FIGURE IT OUT.**

Some ponies get their cutie marks at the exact same time, because they are all connected to one another! Did you know that's how it happened for the CUTIE MARK CRUSADERS?

When they got their cutie marks, they discovered that what sets them apart from other ponies is also what BRINGS THEM TOGETHER.

There's no forcing it. **CUTIE MARKS JUST HAPPEN** when they happen. It's very natural.

When cutie marks do happen, they always turn
out perfectly. And all the fear and stress ponies
may have felt just fade away.

But cutie mark magic doesn't stop there! Ponies have to be careful! They could get a bad case of

CUTIE POX.

That's when ponies break out in **RANDOM CUTIE MARKS** and perform tasks or talents associated with those cutie marks.

Other strange cutie mark magic can make a pony's cutie mark switch with another pony's cutie mark.

TALK ABOUT STRESSFUL!

When that happens, only GOOD FRIENDS CAN HELP a pony get back to normal.

There are even ponies out there who might try to **STEAL CUTIE MARKS** and replace them with something else entirely. So many things can happen with cutie marks!

When it comes to figuring out cutie marks, ponies should just go out and be the best ponies they can be. If they do what they  **LOVE** and follow their  **HEARTS,** magic will do the rest.

Cutie marks are meant to show the world just how unique and special ponies are.

THAT'S THE BEST THING ABOUT CUTIE MARKS!

Today, the Crystal Empire is a beautiful paradise, but it wasn't always so nice. For a long time, the Crystal Empire was under an

EVIL ENCHANTMENT.

A **SUPER BAD PONY** named **KING SOMBRA**
put a spell over the entire kingdom that

MADE IT EVIL.

Then he **ENSLAVED** all the Crystal ponies.

He cursed the Crystal Empire and made it
DISAPPEAR FOR ONE THOUSAND YEARS!
When it finally came back, King Sombra came
back with it.

Princess Celestia and Princess Luna wanted to **DEFEAT KING SOMBRA.** But they knew they needed somepony special to help the Crystal Empire.

Princess Celestia and Princess Luna summoned Princess Cadance and Shining Armor to the Crystal Empire to **PROTECT IT FROM DARKNESS** and save the Crystal ponies.

Protecting the Crystal Empire was exhausting and drained Princess Cadance of all her strength. So Princess Twilight and her best friends came to

HELP!

Princess Twilight Sparkle, Applejack, Fluttershy, Pinkie Pie, Rainbow Dash, and Rarity **ALL WORKED TOGETHER** and figured out that they needed to find the Crystal Heart

TO SAVE THE EMPIRE.

They could use its magic to focus all the LOVE AND LIGHT the Crystal ponies had inside them.

While Princess Cadance and Shining Armor kept protecting everypony, Twilight searched for the

CRYSTAL HEART.

She and Spike **LOOKED HIGH AND LOW,** but they couldn't find it.

In the meantime, Pinkie Pie and the other ponies threw an awesome Crystal Faire as a distraction. They had a flügelhorn and tiny ewes and crystal games, and it was so much fun. Everypony loved it.

EVERYPONY EXCEPT

KING SOMBRA.

Twilight finally FOUND THE CRYSTAL HEART, but King Sombra trapped her! SHE TOSSED THE HEART TO SPIKE.

He tried to get away with it, but he tripped and DROPPED THE HEART! It looked like King Sombra was going to get it and ALL HOPE WAS LOST!

But Shining Armor and Princess Cadance had **NOT LOST HOPE.** Shining Armor picked up Princess Cadance, aimed her like a javelin, **AND THREW HER INTO THE AIR!**

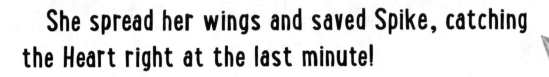

She spread her wings and saved Spike, catching the Heart right at the last minute!

KING SOMBRA WAS DEFEATED!

The Crystal Empire returned to the enchanted kingdom of peace and love that it once was, and all **THE CRYSTAL PONIES CHEERED.**

That is the story of how Princess Cadance and Shining Armor ended up ruling the Crystal Empire, and that is why baby Flurry Heart has the BRAVEST AND MOST AMAZING PARENTS EVER!

HEARTH'S WARMING EVE

AKA KEEP YOUR HOOVSIES WARM!

Every day in Equestria is special.
Some days are special for a specific
reason. **THOSE ARE CALLED
HOLIDAYS!** There are all
kinds of holidays. One of
the ponies' favorites is

HEARTH'S WARMING EVE.

Hearth's Warming Eve is a day when ponies buy presents for other ponies, share delicious sweet things to eat, sing songs, and it's just **THE BEST.**

But it celebrates something very, very serious....

A long time ago, Unicorns, Pegasi, and Earth ponies did not get along.

THEY FOUGHT ABOUT EVERYTHING.

The more the ponies fought,
THE WORSE THE WEATHER GOT.

The ponies didn't realize that strange creatures called **WINDIGOS CAUSED THE BAD WEATHER.**

WINDIGOS ARE SCARY WIND MONSTERS
who feed off anger and turn it into cold and snow.

With all the fighting going on among ponies, the

**WINDIGOS ALMOST FROZE
EVERYPONY FOR GOOD!**

The Earth ponies, Unicorns, and Pegasi huddled around a **TINY HEARTH FOR WARMTH.**

They started to
SING SONGS AND TELL STORIES.

Then they realized they **WEREN'T THAT DIFFERENT FROM ONE ANOTHER.**

Their new warmth for one another ignited **THE FIRE OF FRIENDSHIP.** The fire warmed them. It warmed the land.

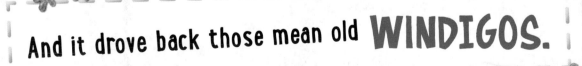

And it drove back those mean old **WINDIGOS.**

They all decided to live together in harmony, and they named the place

EQUESTRIA!

That's where all the ponies live today! And that is why ponies all sing songs, share food, and give presents on Hearth's Warming Eve.

They're **CELEBRATING** the magic of their **FRIENDSHIP** that keeps them all feeling warm and loved and safe.

NIGHTMARE NIGHT

AKA SPOOOOOOKY!

BOO!

PRINCESS LUNA is Princess Celestia's little sister and responsible for using her magic to bring out the moon every night. She is kind and wise, but she wasn't always the sweet, friendly princess everypony knows her to be.

SHE USED TO BE VERY DIFFERENT!

A long time ago, she grew very jealous that ponies played during the day but slept through the beautiful night that she created for them.

She got angry with her sister, Celestia, and transformed herself into

NIGHTMARE MOON.

She wanted to punish everypony by making it **STAY NIGHT FOREVER!**

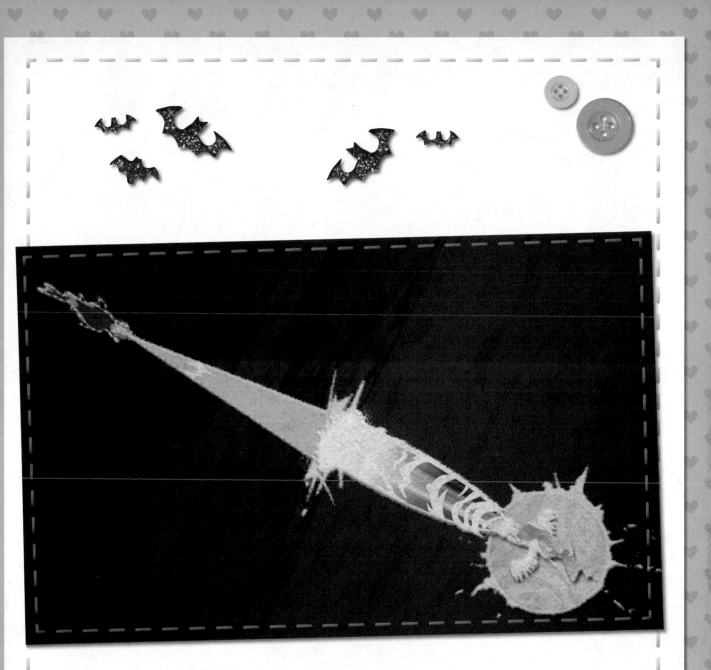

As Nightmare Moon,

SHE COULD DO JUST THAT.

Celestia was forced to trap her sister in the

MOON

for a thousand years!

Soon, the story of Nightmare Moon became something that ponies would tell colts and fillies around campfires and at bedtime to **SCARE THEM.**

Eventually, ponies created a whole holiday to celebrate the story of Nightmare Moon.

THEY CALL IT NIGHTMARE NIGHT.

On Nightmare Night, ponies DRESS UP in all kinds of amazing costumes. They go out to parties and PLAY GAMES AND EAT SWEETS.

One time, **PINKIE PIE DRESSED UP LIKE A CHICKEN.** Lots of ponies thought it was the best costume ever!

PINKIE PIE WAS PRETTY PROUD.

Nightmare Night is a night for telling

SPOOKY STORIES

and pulling **PRANKS.**

Everypony gets really scared but in a fun way! Pranksters like Pinkie Pie and Rainbow Dash have

THE GREATEST TIME.

When Princess Luna finally came back from being banished to the moon, she learned about Nightmare Night and GOT VERY SAD.

Her feelings were hurt because there was a whole holiday all about ponies being scared of her.

Twilight Sparkle showed Luna that all everypony likes to be a little scared. It's all part of the fun!

Well, everypony
EXCEPT FLUTTERSHY.

Now ponies still **ENJOY NIGHTMARE NIGHT.** They still dress up in costumes and scare other ponies and get candy, but they also celebrate it because Nightmare Moon is gone and they have Princess Luna back.

AND THAT IS A GREAT THING TO CELEBRATE.

EQUESTRIA

AKA
LAND OF HARMONY!

EQUESTRIA is such a **FUN PLACE** to live and to explore. There are so many different places with so many different kinds of ponies.

There's the beauty and majesty of **CANTERLOT**. That's where Princess Luna and Celestia live. It's also where they hold the **GRAND GALLOPING GALA** every year to **CELEBRATE THE BUILDING OF CANTERLOT.**

There are also the simple charms of PONYVILLE. Some would say that Ponyville is the heart of Equestria.

IT'S CERTAINLY WHERE SOME OF THE COOLEST PONIES LIVE!

That includes Princess Twilight Sparkle, Pinkie Pie, Rainbow Dash, Applejack, Fluttershy, and Rarity!

Right next door to Ponyville, there's the magic and mystery of the **EVERFREE FOREST.**

Nopony knows all its secrets—well, except maybe Zecora.

If it's hustle and bustle a pony craves, he or she need look no further than **MANEHATTAN.**

That's where to find the latest fashions or catch a show on Bridleway.

Rough-and-tumble ponies can head on out to **APPLELOOSA,** where the ponies and Buffalo have learned to share the land together. Spend time at the Salt Block saloon, catch a musical performance, or enjoy the acres and acres of apple orchards.

Ponies who can fly can head on up to **CLOUDSDALE** to see how the Pegasi make clouds, snow, and rainbows at the weather factory. The whole city is made of clouds.

Speaking of rainbows, there's the swap meet at **RAINBOW FALLS**. Ponies can always find what they're looking for there—like rare books and fun knickknacks!

Lucky ponies may get to go visit the Griffons in their home, **GRIFFONSTONE**. They should be careful not to sing while there, since it is not allowed!

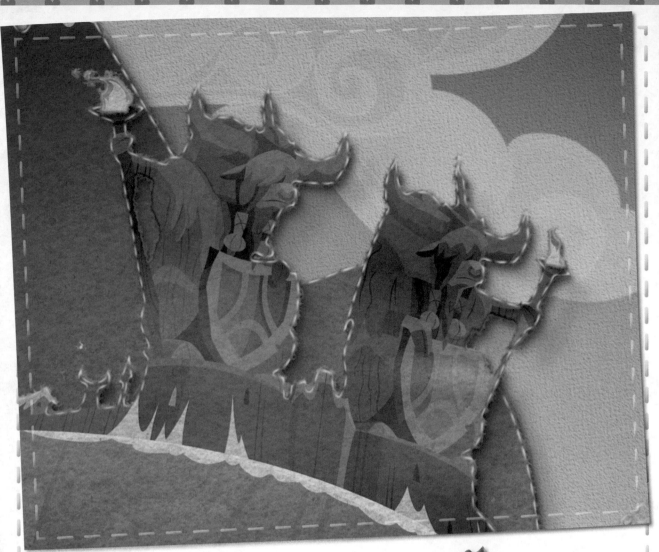

Or they can go north
and see the Yaks in
YAKYAKISTAN. That's
where Prince Rutherford
rules. He can be a little
short-tempered. One time
he visited Ponyville and
busted up everything!

There's **LAS PEGASUS.** It's a loud and colorful city in the clouds. They love to have parties there. Ponies like to visit for fun rides, games, stage shows, and amazing food.

Art lovers and foodies love to visit big cities like **BALTIMARE.**

History buffs

FLOCK TO FILLYDELPHIA!

VANHOOVER has stunning views of mountains and the ocean.

NEIGHAGRA FALLS is a refreshing tourist spot where ponies can take boat rides, swim, or just enjoy the view of one of the biggest waterfalls in Equestria.

There are tons of other great places in Equestria! There are always going to be **NEW PLACES TO EXPLORE** for an adventurous pony. And what do new places have? **NEW FRIENDS!**

APPLEWOOD

THE CRYSTALLING

AKA FLURRY HEART GOES BOOM!

When Flurry Heart was born, the Crystal Empire had the

BIGGEST CRYSTALLING EVER.

A **CRYSTALLING** is when all the ponies in the Crystal Empire gather around the **CRYSTAL HEART** and see a **NEW BABY** for the very first time.

The **LOVE** from all the ponies **FLOWS INTO THE HEART**, making it even stronger so it can **PROTECT THE WHOLE EMPIRE.**

Things didn't go quite so smoothly for

FLURRY HEART'S
CRYSTALLING.

When all the ponies showed up, Flurry Heart's dad, Shining Armor, was just so TIRED from taking care of a new baby. Princess Cadance wasn't sure what to do.

Flurry Heart could already FLY like a Wonderbolt and use MAGIC like a much older Unicorn. She was quite the hoof-ful for new parents.

Keeping her under control was tough enough, but then she **ACCIDENTALLY** used her magic to **BLAST** the Crystal Heart into a **MILLION TINY PIECES!**

THINGS GOT REALLY BAD.

Without the Heart, a **HUGE STORM BEGAN TO GATHER.** The cold and windy dangerous weather of the north **THREATENED EVERYPONY** in the Empire.

All the Crystal ponies who came to the Crystalling were so excited to meet Flurry Heart that they didn't let the bad weather drive them away.

They wanted to show their

LOVE AND SUPPORT
FOR FLURRY HEART.

Princess Twilight Sparkle thought she found a spell book that could help, but then Flurry Heart's magic got out of control and she

ACCIDENTALLY DISINTEGRATED IT.

A Unicorn named Sunburst figured out just what to do.
He knew magic very well and he had the idea for Starlight
Glimmer, Shining Armor, and the princesses to focus their

LOVE AND MAGIC

 INTO REPAIRING THE HEART.

Thanks to Sunburst, **THE CRYSTAL HEART WAS RESTORED,** Flurry Heart's magic calmed down...

It was one of the most

AMAZING CRYSTALLINGS

in the history of the Crystal Empire.

THE MAGIC OF FRIENDSHIP

AKA FRIENDS ARE AWESOME!

There are a lot of things colts and fillies may experience as they grow up:

attending a wedding,

foal-sitting little ones,

meeting an Alicorn,

getting a cutie mark,

celebrating Hearth's Warming Eve and Nightmare Night,

exploring Equestria,

but most IMPORTANT...

...HAVING FRIENDS! Princess Twilight Sparkle, Pinkie Pie, Fluttershy, Applejack, Rainbow Dash, and Rarity are **EXPERTS ON FRIENDSHIP**. But that wasn't always the case.

Twilight Sparkle brought them all together and taught them a lot. And they taught her a lot. Then they taught one another a lot!

THAT'S HOW FRIENDSHIP IS SUPPOSED TO WORK.

IT'S EASY TO MAKE FRIENDS EVERYWHERE IN EQUESTRIA, but there are some things to keep in mind along the way when making new friends.

First, ponies should **ALWAYS BE KIND** to anypony they meet. No matter how they are treated in return, there is always room for **KINDNESS**.

PONIES SHOULD BE GENEROUS. They can let other ponies know they are valued.

They should
ALWAYS BE
HONEST.

It might be hard sometimes,
but ponies appreciate a friend who
can **TELL THEM HOW IT IS.**

Ponies should **ALWAYS BE LOYAL** to those **PONIES THEY TRUST.**

They can always be there for
them through thick and thin.

Finally, ponies should always remember laughter.
When times get tough, it's good to have a friend
who can BRING ON THE LAUGHS.

If a pony can do all that, then **THE MAGIC OF HAVING FRIENDS WILL ALWAYS BE THERE** and help them share the joys, pains, and everything in between.

The End

...FOR NOW!